PEOPLE & PLACES

Israel

Written by

Marilyn Tolhurst

Consultant Burt Keimach

Illustrated by

Ann Savage and Linden Hamilton

SILVER BURDETT PRESS
ENGLEWOOD CLIFFS, NEW JERSEY

Series Editor Sue Seddon
U.S. Project Editor Nancy Furstinger
Designer Robert Mathias, Publishing Workshop
Photo-researcher Hugh Olliff

A TEMPLAR BOOK

Devised and produced by Templar Publishing Ltd
107 High Street, Dorking, Surrey RH4 1QA

Adapted and first published in the United States in 1989
by Silver Burdett Press, Englewood Cliffs, N.J.

Color separations by Positive Colour Ltd, Maldon, Essex
Printed by L.E.G.O., Vicenza, Italy

Library of Congress Cataloging-in-Publication Data

Tolhurst, Marilyn.
    Israel / written by Marilyn Tolhurst; illustrated by Ann Savage.
        p. cm. — (People & places)
    "A Templar book"—T.p. verso.
    Includes index.
    Summary: Text and illustrations introduce the geography, history,
people, and culture of Israel.
    1. Israel—Juvenile literature.   [1. Israel.]   I. Savage, Ann, ill.
II. Title. III. Series: People & places (Englewood Cliffs, N.J.)
DS102.95.T65   1988
956.94'06—dc 19   88-30070
ISBN 0-382-09830-7   CIP
                                                          AC

Contents

WHERE IN THE WORLD?

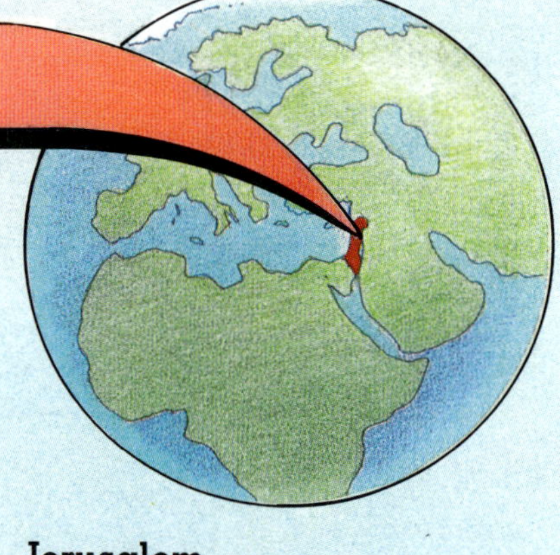

Israel lies on the eastern shore of the Mediterranean where Europe, Asia, and Africa meet. It is one of the world's newest countries. Israel was created in 1948 from a land called Palestine as a country in which Jewish people could live. Despite its small size it contains a variety of scenery, ranging from fertile farmland to desert.

During its long history the region has been an important trading place and a link between East and West. It is the land where the Jews of the Bible lived thousands of years ago and the land where Christianity began. It is also the home of many Arab Muslims and Christians.

When Israel became a country for the Jewish people after World War II, the Arabs, who were also living there, objected. So did the governments of neighboring Arab countries. It is a problem that has never been resolved and is generally known as the Arab-Israeli problem.

Today Israel governs territories captured in wars with the neighboring countries of Egypt, Jordan, Syria, and Lebanon. These include the West Bank, the Gaza Strip, and the Golan Heights.

Jerusalem

Jerusalem is the capital city of Israel and the seat of government. Many countries, however, regard Tel Aviv as the capital. Jerusalem is also a great historical and religious center, important to Jews, Christians, and Muslims alike.

Symbols of Israel

The flag is blue and white to resemble a Jewish prayer shawl, worn at religious services, called a *tallit*. In the center is the ancient symbol of the Jews, the Shield of David.

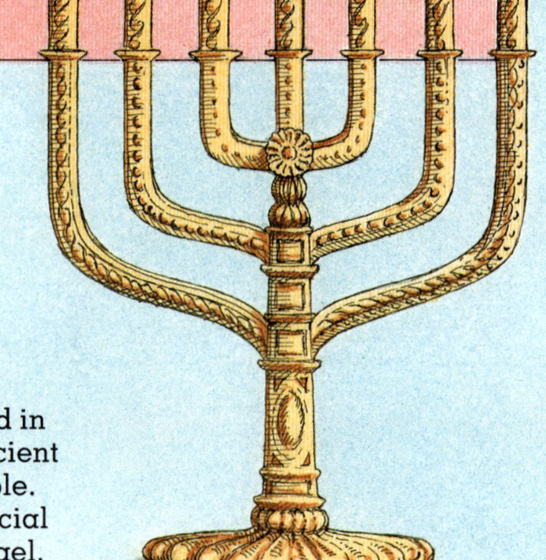

The Menorah, a seven branched candlestick used in the Temple, is another ancient symbol of the Jewish people. Today it is used as the official emblem of the State of Israel.

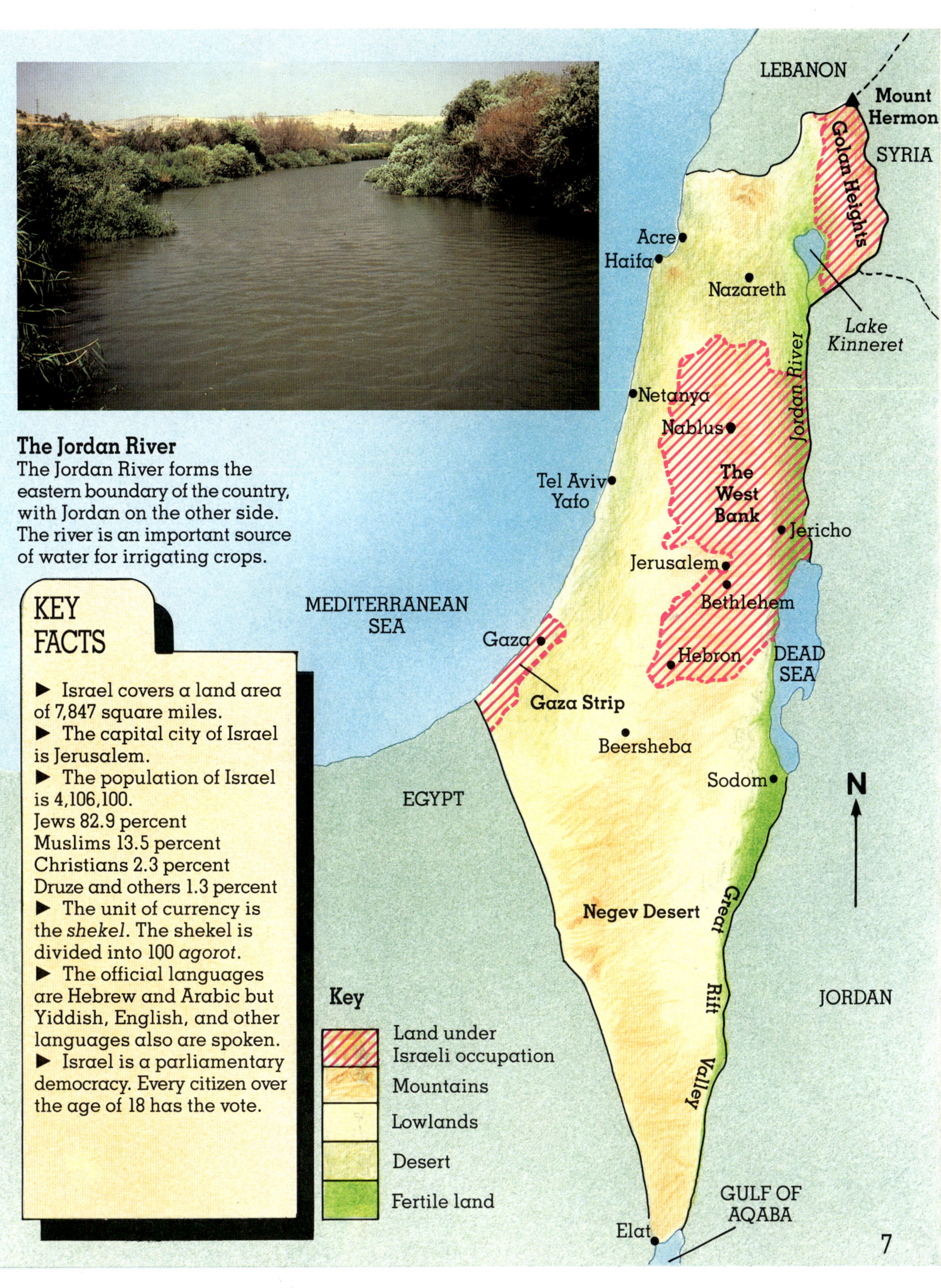

The Jordan River

The Jordan River forms the eastern boundary of the country, with Jordan on the other side. The river is an important source of water for irrigating crops.

KEY FACTS

► Israel covers a land area of 7,847 square miles.
► The capital city of Israel is Jerusalem.
► The population of Israel is 4,106,100.
Jews 82.9 percent
Muslims 13.5 percent
Christians 2.3 percent
Druze and others 1.3 percent
► The unit of currency is the *shekel*. The shekel is divided into 100 *agorot*.
► The official languages are Hebrew and Arabic but Yiddish, English, and other languages also are spoken.
► Israel is a parliamentary democracy. Every citizen over the age of 18 has the vote.

Key

Land under Israeli occupation
Mountains
Lowlands
Desert
Fertile land

DESERTS, MOUNTAINS, PLAINS

Israel is a small country. At its longest point from north to south it measures only 310 miles, and it is possible to drive the length of the country in a day. Nowhere is it wider than 62 miles, yet within its borders the landscape varies widely.

A long backbone of mountains runs from north to south and includes the rugged hills of Galilee, Samaria, and Judea. Much of this land is dusty and barren with only scrub vegetation. It is the "wilderness" mentioned in the Bible.

The Great Rift Valley was formed when two plates in the Earth's surface moved apart. It begins in Syria and ends in East Africa, running the length of Israel on its eastern edge. It is the deepest valley on Earth. The northern part of it was once swampland. It has now been drained and is an agricultural area and also a nature reserve. Farther south the Jordan River runs through it. The Dead Sea lies in the Rift Valley on the edge of the Negev Desert. Many parts of the Negev have been successfully developed for agriculture. The plain that stretches along the edge of the Mediterranean Sea is fertile farmland where many people live.

Sun
Israel's coastline has a pleasant Mediterranean climate and is a popular vacation resort for Israelis and foreign tourists alike. Rain only falls between the months of November and April. Dry desert winds sometimes blow in during the spring and autumn, making the temperature soar.

Sand
The Negev Desert is an arid region of wind-blown earth and limestone mountains. It covers 60 percent of Israel's total area. Rain rarely falls and in summer the Negev shimmers with heat. For centuries the only people who used it were the Bedouins who grazed their sheep and goats on the edges. Today, attempts are being made to mine it for minerals. Parts of the desert have been successfully irrigated. Israeli scientists have discovered millions of cubic feet of water beneath it.

Water

Water, or the lack of it, is a major concern in Israel. The major source of water is the Jordan River and Lake Kinneret, and there are canals and pipelines that carry water to the dry south. New methods of taking the salt out of seawater to make it drinkable and of recycling sewage water are being developed to increase the water supply. Lake Kinneret, seen here, is a major recreation area as well as a reservoir.

Salt

The Dead Sea is the lowest point on Earth and is 1,296 feet below sea level. It is eight times as salty as ordinary seawater. Although the Jordan River flows into it, it cannot flow out again because the Dead Sea is below the surrounding land. The trapped water evaporates in the heat and leaves salt and other minerals behind.

► Mount Hermon, on the border with Syria, is Israel's highest mountain. It is 9,286 feet high and the source of the Jordan River.
► Winter snowfalls are not unusual in the mountain areas.
► More than 2,500 different plants grow in Israel. Of these 150 grow only in Israel.
► Winter temperatures range between 43°F in Jerusalem and 50°F in Elat. In summer, temperatures range between 82°F in Jerusalem and 103°F in Elat.

TEEMING WILDLIFE

Ibex

Within Israel's boundaries the Mediterranean region meets the desert. There is a band of scrub country in between. These three natural zones provide habitats for a huge variety of wildlife and plants.

The poets of the Bible described Israel as a land of wheat and barley and vines, of fig trees and pomegranates, of olive trees and honey bees. Today these plants and animals still flourish in the Mediterranean climate.

In the scrublands and mountains the animal life includes gazelle and ibex (a kind of wild goat), lizards, and snakes. There are now 280 wildlife reserves that protect some of Israel's rare or endangered species such as the leopard and the vulture. Special feeding stations have been set up for wolves, hyenas, and foxes. On the coast, the eggs of turtles are regularly collected and hatched in incubators and the young turtles returned to the Mediterranean.

The desert blooms in February and March when plants such as groundsel and dandelion flower. Tough terebinth and acacia trees, some of them hundreds of years old, send up new shoots each year as their roots search deeply for every available drop of moisture.

Flying visitors

In autumn and spring the skies of Israel teem with migrating birds. The country is at a junction of northern and southern breeding areas of the world and many birds pass through it on their long seasonal journeys. Flocks of white storks can be seen feeding in the autumn before continuing on their way to their winter quarters in southern Africa.

Storks

Lizard

New for old

In two special wildlife reserves there is a project to reintroduce certain animals which were mentioned in the Bible but which have since become extinct in the region. Now, ostriches, wild donkeys, Persian fallow deer, and other species are being bred, to be set free at a future date.

Ostriches

Wild donkeys

A carpet of flowers

In spring, the landscape in the north becomes a carpet of blossoms. Wild irises, lilies, tulips, hyacinths, and anemones make a breathtaking show of color. All Israelis, from the smallest child, know that it is forbidden to pick these national treasures.

11

NEW NATION, OLD ROOTS

Jews have lived in the region that is now Israel for thousands of years. However, during the Roman occupation of Palestine (now Israel), more than 2,000 years ago, many Jews fled abroad to escape Roman rule. Over the centuries they settled in many countries throughout the world. Eventually there were more Jews living outside Palestine than in it. However, there have always been some Jews living in Palestine.

The Jews took their religion and customs with them into exile and never forgot where they had come from. Generations of Jews grew up in countries far away but still regarded Palestine as their homeland. Many longed to return and to have a country of their own. By the end of the 19th century this dream became a reality for some Jews from Eastern Europe who settled in Palestine (see page 22).

Many Jews followed their example and returned to their homeland. In 1948 Palestine became the independent state of Israel (see page 22). By 1953 Israel's Jewish population had doubled through immigration.

Today the population of Israel is a mixture of people from more than 70 different countries. They include the Palestinian Arabs who already lived in Israel when the Jews began to return.

The Bedouin

Ten percent of Israel's Arab population are Bedouins. Most of them live in the desert region and some still live a traditional nomadic way of life, following their grazing herds. However, they are beginning to live a more settled way of life and many now dwell in villages and work as laborers and factory workers. Some have attended college and succeeded in medicine, law, and other professions.

New arrivals

Although immigration into Israel is slowing down, many Jews from countries as far off as India and Australia, Ethiopia and the Yemen are still arriving to make a new life there. When they are allowed, Russian Jews also emigrate to Israel. The government offers financial assistance and help with housing and employment.

Sabras

Sabra (right) is the name given to Jews born in Israel, who are rapidly developing a sense of national identity. A sabra is a kind of cactus which grows all over the country. The fruit is prickly on the outside but soft and sweet within. This is thought to be a good description of the native-born Israeli character.

Palestinian Arabs

The Palestinian Arabs who stayed in Israel after independence have full rights as citizens of the country. Today they call themselves Israeli Arabs. However, many Palestinian Arabs fled from Israel at independence. They went to live in areas close to Israel which were under Arab control. In 1967 these areas – the Gaza Strip and the West Bank – were occupied by the Israelis and are now under Israeli control. Although living standards for the Palestinians in these areas have improved under Israeli rule the Palestinians are discontent. Their sense of injustice at not having a country of their own is a problem both nationally and internationally. Here Palestinian Arabs relax in the West Bank.

The Druzes

The Druzes (left) are a close-knit religious group whose beliefs are based on Islamic teaching. They believe very firmly in their religion and do not intermarry with other groups. They have been established in the country for 800 years. They speak Arabic. There are many Druzes in top positions in the government and the military.

BUILDING THE NATION

After independence, the Israelis had a lot of work to do. With millions of new citizens and few natural resources, everyone had to work hard to build a new nation. Help came and continues to come from Jewish communities in America and Europe who contribute large sums of money towards the country's needs. The United States government also provides development aid and loans.

The country's economy was gradually changed into the modern system that exists today. The economy is based on industry – especially on food products, textiles and clothing, chemicals, rubber, and plastic that are produced in factories across the land.

Every effort has been made to utilize the raw materials that are available. The Dead Sea minerals of potash, salt, lime, and magnesium are an important source of wealth. The country is now a world leader in high technology products. Medical and agricultural electronics, telecommunications, and computer hardware are important areas of production.

Women workers
Israel has a shortage of skilled labor and works hard to train the workforce in the new technologies on which its economy depends. The Middle East is traditionally an area where women do not work alongside men, but in Israel more and more women are taking jobs outside the home. Today they form 36 percent of the workforce.

High technology
Israel is very advanced in the field of high technology. Israeli scientists have developed robots, computer "brains," pilotless planes, nuclear power, laser surgery, and computer assisted scanners for looking into the body. A computerized tractor, which is modeled on a tank and has wheels like those of a lunar probe vehicle, also has been developed.

Solar energy

Israel is a world leader in the development of solar energy (using heat from the sun). About one quarter of all households have solar waterheat and it is now a law that all new houses have this system. Some companies have solar heating equipment for running machinery. In 1983 the first of a number of solar energy power stations was built on the shores of the Dead Sea. These stations can work at night and in winter because solar energy is stored in the very salty pools (right).

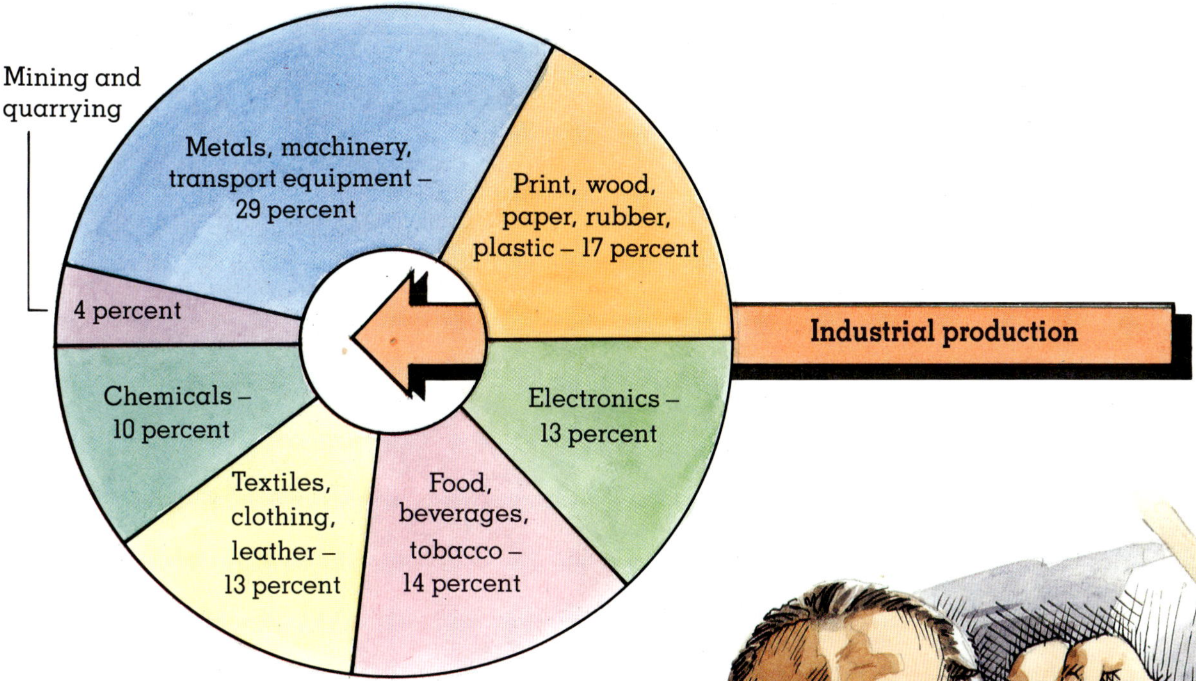

Mining and quarrying

Metals, machinery, transport equipment – 29 percent

Print, wood, paper, rubber, plastic – 17 percent

4 percent

Chemicals – 10 percent

Electronics – 13 percent

Textiles, clothing, leather – 13 percent

Food, beverages, tobacco – 14 percent

Industrial production

Polished diamonds

Diamond polishing is an important industry in Israel. It produces 80 percent of the world's output of small polished diamonds – the kind that are used in jewelry settings. The stones are imported in the rough state and then skillfully cut into all sizes and shapes, and polished.

WORKING THE LAND

Israel grows a variety of crops including cotton and fruits such as bananas, avocado pears, and citrus fruit. The fruit is exported to many parts of the world. Israeli scientists have developed farming technology to transform desert into fertile fields. Israeli irrigation methods are wellknown throughout the world and Israelis have helped many Third World countries to grow crops in dry areas. Israel even manages to grow some crops by watering with salt water, although this is still in an experimental stage.

Israel produces most of the food it needs. Half of it is grown on special farming villages called *kibbutzim*. The word *kibbutz* means "coming together" and the people who live and work on a kibbutz share everything. They work and eat with each other and together make all the decisions about the way in which the kibbutz is run.

The *moshav* is a slightly different method of farming. Here families live separately in their own houses and farm their own land but share the packing transporting, and marketing of their products.

Joining together

The kibbutz is not just a farming village, it is a way of life. It was started at the beginning of the 20th century by people who wanted to build a new society based on equality and justice. Food, housing, education, and health care are all supplied by the kibbutz. Routine jobs such as cleaning, cooking, and serving meals are shared by everyone. During the day babies and children under school age are looked after in a children's house. Here *kibbutzniks*, or people who live on a kibbutz, work on a kibbutz near Gaza.

Golden harvest

Citrus fruits, such as oranges, are one of the main products of Israel's agriculture. Citrus groves are a common sight in the northern half of the country where the climate suits their cultivation. The best of the fruit is exported under the Israeli trade name *Jaffa*. Much of it finds its way to European markets. Some of the fruit is pressed for its juice.

Drip by drip

Nearly half the country's farmland is under irrigation. A revolutionary system of drip-irrigation has been developed which provides moisture directly to the roots of plants without any waste of precious water. This has led to a great increase in production. Some of the irrigation systems are computer-operated.

LAND OF THE BIBLE

The story of the Jewish people is closely bound up with the land of Israel which they regard as their ancient homeland. The Hebrew Bible (the Old Testament books of the Christian Bible) records their early history; and it is read in Israeli schools today both as a history book and as a holy book. Abraham, about whom there are stories in the Bible, is regarded as the father of the nation. He was probably the leader of a nomadic tribe who made a great journey in ancient times across the desert from Mesopotamia (now Iraq) to the land of Canaan (now Israel).

Many years later, during a famine, Abraham's descendants went to live in Egypt where there was more food. Here they were treated as slaves but were eventually led to freedom by Moses, the great leader of the Jewish people. According to the Bible, God gave Moses the Law by which the Jews were to live. From then on the Law was developed so that there were rules covering most aspects of daily life such as food, the family, and property.

Under the leadership of Joshua, the Israelites settled in Canaan and made it successful. In the 11th century BC they elected Saul as their first king. He was succeeded by David, who fought Goliath and founded Jerusalem, and then by Solomon, who was famous for his wisdom. Troubled times followed, ending with the Roman occupation of the land to which they gave the name Palestine.

The Dead Sea Scrolls

In 1947 some shepherd boys discovered a collection of ancient scrolls (books written on rolls of very fine animal skin called parchment) in caves at Qumran near the Dead Sea. They are thought to be part of a library belonging to an ancient Jewish community called the Essenes. Some of them date from the 3rd century BC. They are one of the most important archaeological finds of this century because they help us to understand more about biblical history and the relationship of the Jews and the Christians.

The oldest church

According to the Bible's New Testament books, Bethlehem (now in the occupied West Bank) was the place where Jesus was born. The site of his birth was marked two centuries later by the Church of the Nativity. This church, rebuilt in the 6th century, is now the oldest Christian church in the world. It is a place of pilgrimage for Christians from all over the world.

The Torah

The Torah consists of the first five books of the Hebrew Bible. The Torah is read and studied by religious Jews everywhere. Each Sabbath (Saturday, the Jewish holy day) a section is read to worshipers in the synagogue (Jewish place of worship). The Torah is important because it contains God's Law and some of the best-known stories in the Bible such as Noah's Ark.

The oldest city

Jericho (above) is an oasis city on the west side of the Jordan River. It is famous in biblical history as the place where Joshua made the walls fall down by a blast on his trumpet. In the 1950s, the site of ancient Jericho was found near the source of an ancient spring. Excavation proved that settlement on the site had been continuous from about 9000 BC, making Jericho one of the oldest-known cities in the world.

19

INVADERS AND CRUSADERS

For centuries Israel has been a land of struggle. Its position at the junction of Europe, Africa, and Asia was important because whoever held it also controlled trade routes between East and West. Alexander the Great invaded the area in 333 BC and for 200 years the Greeks ruled the land. Then the expanding Roman Empire took it over in 63 BC, crushing all resistance, and, succeeded by the Byzantines (the Christian Roman Empire), held power in the region for almost 600 years. During this period many Jews fled into exile. As the strength of the Byzantines declined, the Arabs conquered Palestine in AD 638. Through most of the succeeding centuries Arabs and Jews lived there together peacefully.

However, Israel was the birthplace of Christianity, and European Christians in the Middle Ages wanted the land to be freed from the Muslims. Eight times between 1095 and 1500, Christian armies began holy wars or Crusades to regain the territory. They succeeded in capturing much of biblical Israel but only held it briefly.

In the 16th century Palestine (now Israel) became part of the Turkish Ottoman Empire and remained so until the end of World War I when it came under British control.

Saladin

Richard I

Saladin and the Lionheart

Saladin was a great Muslim warrior of the 12th century. In 1187 he captured Jerusalem. This led to the Third Crusade, headed by King Richard I of England, known as the Lionheart for his bravery in battle. Richard wanted to regain Jerusalem in the name of Christianity but met his match in Saladin. The Crusade ended in a truce and Richard withdrew, but first he made the Muslims agree that the holy places of Jerusalem should be open to Christian pilgrims.

The city walls

The old city of Jerusalem is surrounded by stone walls built 400 years ago by Suleiman the Magnificent, the Turkish sultan who ruled the Ottoman Empire. There are eight gates in the wall. The Damascus Gate marks the start of the road leading to that city. The Lions' Gate (left) is named after the carved lions in the wall on each side and the Dung Gate is so called because it was where refuse was thrown out of the city.

Last stand against Rome

Masada is a mountain stronghold on the shores of the Dead Sea. Its top was fortified by King Herod the Great in the years when Israel was under Roman domination. It was the site of the last stand of a band of Jews who were strongly against Roman rule. When the Romans besieged it in AD 72, nearly 1,000 of the Jewish defenders committed suicide rather than surrender.

THE PROMISED LAND

By the 19th century many of the Jews who were scattered throughout the world began to long for a country of their own. This idea became a movement called Zionism. The thoughts of the Zionists turned to Palestine, the land where their ancestors had lived centuries before. In the late 19th century the first group of Jews traveled from Europe to Palestine and settled there. More followed, and by 1936 about 250,000 Jewish immigrants had settled in Palestine.

However, the Jews did not gain their promised land easily. The Palestinian Arabs who already lived there were extremely unhappy about the increasing numbers of Jewish immigrants settling in Palestine and rioted several times. The British, who ruled Palestine from 1917, supported the idea of Zionism at first. However, as Arab unrest grew, the British leaders became divided on whether to support the Arabs or the Jews and how to solve the problem.

In 1947, after mounting violence from both Jews and Arabs, the British asked the United Nations (UN) to find a solution to the Arab-Jewish problem. That year the UN approved a plan to divide Palestine into two separate states, one Arab, one Jewish. The Jews accepted this idea but the Arabs rejected it and the Arab state planned by the UN never came about. Eventually Israel decided to declare itself an independent state and did so on May 14, 1948.

Zionism

Theodor Herzl (1860-1904) was a Jewish journalist who lived in Austria in the 19th century. He was not religious but he became convinced that Jews would never find peace until they had a country of their own. He turned the movement known as Zionism (after Mount Zion in Jerusalem) from a group of small societies into an international organization and became its leader. Zionists wanted there to be a Jewish state in Palestine again.

Ghetto life

Although the Jews lived in Europe for centuries they were not welcome. They were persecuted for their religious beliefs and for their way of life. They were often forced to live separately from other citizens in ghettos. These were parts of cities, often walled around and shut at night, where Jews had to live in cramped and unhealthy conditions. This depicts a ghetto in Eastern Europe.

Catastrophe

The worst persecution of Jews in Europe happened during World War II when German Nazis set out to kill them all in death camps such as Auschwitz and Treblinka. Six million Jews were killed. This terrible happening, known as the Holocaust, made the Jews in Palestine even more determined to hold on to their land. This memorial (right) to the victims of the camps is at Yad Veshem, Israel.

Pioneers

These Jewish immigrants below, arriving in Palestine by ship in 1947, were hoping for a new life. However, conditions were usually harsh. The land on which they settled was often swamp or desert and they had to work extremely hard to develop it into fertile farmland. They also worked to create a society that was based on fairness and hard work.

STRIFE AND CHANGING BOUNDARIES

Israel was born into war. Within 24 hours of becoming a nation it was attacked by the combined forces of neighboring Arab states. The Israelis fought back. In 1949 there was a ceasefire. Israel had taken over some of the territory that the United Nations had planned as a state for the Palestinian Arabs; Arab states had taken over the rest: Jordan held the West Bank and half of Jerusalem and Egypt held the Gaza Strip. The Arab state planned by the UN did not come about. Thousands of Palestinian Arabs were homeless and had to live in refugee camps. The question of the Palestinian refugees and their lack of their own homeland is the root of the hostility between the state of Israel and most of the Arab states today.

The Israelis have rarely been able to live in peace. In 1967 war with Egypt and other Arab states broke out. The June War, or the Six Day War as it is known by Israelis, ended in victory for the Israelis. They captured the remaining part of their holy city of Jerusalem and the West Bank from Jordan, the Golan Heights from Syria, and Sinai and the Gaza Strip from Egypt.

More Palestinians were made homeless and moved into refugee camps. As their sense of injustice grew, some of them began to use guerrilla warfare, setting ambushes and making surprise attacks against the Israelis. Their guerrilla groups were based in the neighboring country of Lebanon. In response to these attacks Israel bombed guerrilla bases in Lebanon and in 1982 invaded Lebanon and drove the Palestinian guerrillas out. Israel has withdrawn from Sinai and Lebanon, but most of the Arab world does not recognize the existence of the state of Israel and the Arab-Israeli problem is not solved.

Ben-Gurion 1886-1973
David Ben-Gurion was Israel's first prime minister. He emigrated to Palestine in 1906 and was a fierce fighter for a Jewish state.

The PLO
The Palestine Liberation Organization is a political and military group founded in 1964. It represents the Palestinian Arabs. The leader of the PLO is Yasser Arafat (above). Other groups exist within the PLO, some of whom pursue their cause with hijacks and attacks on Israeli targets.

History is made

In 1977, the president of Egypt, Anwar Sadat, went to Israel to meet the prime minister, Menachem Begin, (below) to try to find a path towards peace. It was the first time that a leader of an Arab country had set foot in Israel. Israel promised to return some of the land gained from Egypt in the June War. The visit led to the Camp David Accords in 1978, when peace was signed between Israel and Egypt.

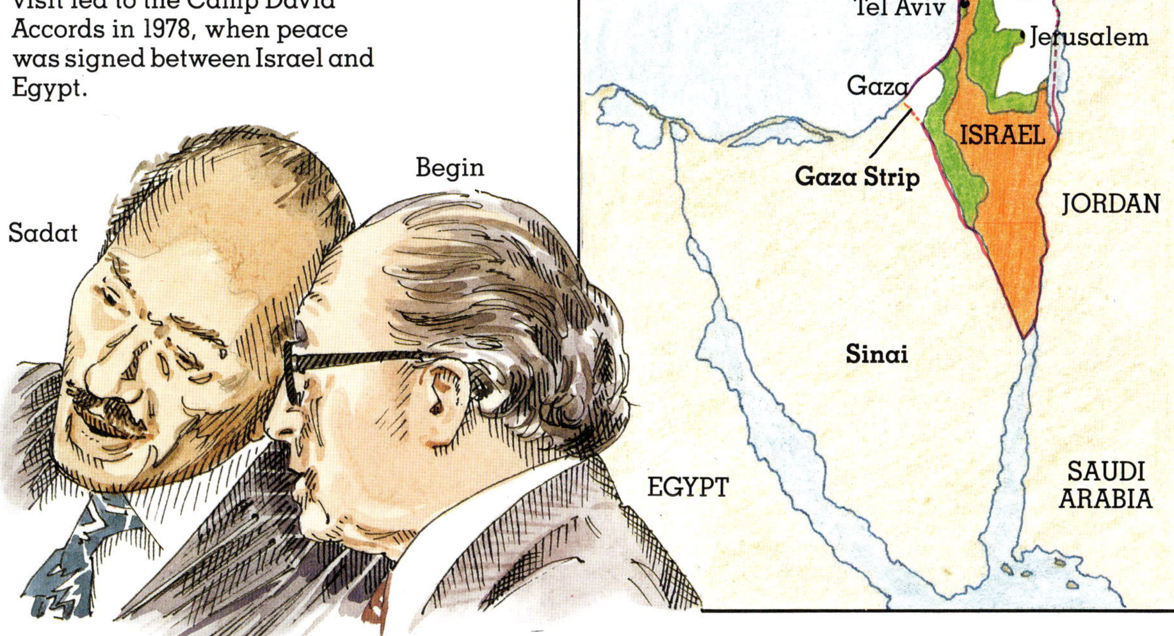

Sadat

Begin

Camp life

Two million Palestinian Arabs live in refugee camps in the Israeli occupied West Bank and Gaza areas and in the neighboring countries of Jordan, Syria, and Lebanon. They come from the area in which the Israeli state was established in 1948. Some families have been living as refugees for 40 years. The United Nations provides aid, education, and health services. The camps are overcrowded and sometimes without the basic essentials of life, such as running water. The conditions cause unrest and sometimes violence.

ISRAEL TODAY

Israel today is a thriving Western-style country with a mixture of peoples and styles of life. It is a parliamentary democracy, which means that all citizens can vote for the political parties they want to represent them. There are two main parties, Labor and Likud (conservative) but so far neither one has ever had a clear majority in parliament so the country is governed by a coalition (joining) of the two.

The army plays a large part in Israeli life since the country has been repeatedly at war with the neighboring states and is constantly on the alert against guerrilla attacks. At 18, Israeli men have to serve a minimum of three years in the army. Israeli women also serve for a term of two years. After that, both men and women must do periods of duty each year. One special army unit is the Nahal. This unit is for young people who choose to do their army service as farmer-soldiers in the border areas.

Arabs may not serve in the army and many of them find the heavy military presence in the country very threatening. Many Israeli Jews would rather not serve in the army but feel that they have no choice until peace is reached.

Many tongues

Israel is a melting pot of different peoples speaking a variety of languages. To make communication easier, Hebrew, as well as Arabic, has been made an official language of the state. Hebrew is the ancient language of the Bible. It has been updated by the addition of modern words. Hebrew has an alphabet of 22 letters and is written from right to left. Books open the opposite way from those written in English and European languages. Most new arrivals to Israel learn Hebrew in special classes.

The Knesset

Members of Israel's parliament, called the Knesset from a Hebrew word meaning "assembly," are voted in every four years. Everyone over the age of 18 has the vote. Debates are conducted in Hebrew but the Arab and Druze members may use Arabic which is the other official language of the state. This is the Knesset in Jerusalem.

Health and welfare

Israel takes good care of its
citizens. There are 145 hospitals
and 870 mother-and-child care
centers. The government owns
some of these and treatment is
free. Other hospitals are private
and some are run by voluntary
organizations. Most people take
out private health insurance.
Israel's doctors have made
important world advances in
areas such as brain surgery,
the treatment of burns, and the
rehabilitation of war victims.
Here a doctor treats a young
patient.

A woman's life?

At the age of 18 women have to
serve two years in the army.
They follow the same training
routine as men although they
no longer join in actual
fighting. Many of them are
instructors in weapon systems,
computers, and driving special
vehicles. Married women with
children, and Druze, Christian,
and Arab women do not have to
serve in the army.

KEEPING IN TOUCH

The Israelis are a very news-conscious people. They read more newspapers than any other nation. As the citizens come from such varied backgrounds, the news must come to them in a number of different languages. Hebrew newspapers and journals can be found on the newsstands right next to those in Arabic and English.

Both radio and television are run by the Israel Broadcasting Authority. Radio broadcasts by the Voice of Israel can be found on five stations; each one has programs for a different kind of audience. New immigrants will find special programs which go out in 12 different languages. One station offers continuous pop music and another, classical music. One station broadcasts entirely in Arabic.

There is one television channel in Israel. About half of the television programs are locally produced. Others are imported from America and Europe and these are usually subtitled in Hebrew and Arabic. Children's programs in the afternoon are followed by two hours of news and features in Arabic. The evening viewing is a mixture of news, sports, light entertainment, and movies.

KEY FACTS

▶ Israel has 15 Hebrew newspapers, five Arabic, and nine in other languages. There are also about 650 magazines.

▶ News broadcasts are made in several languages, including Hebrew, Arabic, English, Yiddish, German, and Russian.

▶ The Defense Forces have a radio station of their own.

▶ Car ownership in Israel has doubled since 1975.

▶ Israel's railroads are important carriers of goods. Passenger use has declined in the last 10 years.

▶ Israel has three deep-water harbors, at Haifa in the north, Ashdod on the south Mediterranean coast, and Elat on the Red Sea.

▶ Israel is connected to the international communications systems by means of underwater cables and communications satellites.

Getting around
During the last 10 years, 2,500 miles of new roads have been built in Israel. Existing roads also have been improved by widening and adding new signs and markings. Traffic travels on the right and all road signs are written in Hebrew, Arabic, and English.

King Solomon's port

The deep-water port at Elat (above) at the head of the Red Sea is both ancient and modern. In biblical times King Solomon used it to export copper from the mines in the Negev and to import gold and other luxuries from Africa. Modern Israelis have rebuilt the port and still use it to export the mining products of the Negev and to import oil.

Flying colors

Israel's national airline is called El Al. International flights operate from the Ben-Gurion Airport at Lod near Tel Aviv. The other main airports are at Jerusalem and Elat. Domestic airlines operate services between the main cities.

LIVING AND LEARNING

David is a sabra which means he was born in Israel. His parents emigrated there from Australia shortly before he was born. They live together in an apartment in Tel Aviv and both of David's parents work in the city.

He goes to a new primary school close to his home where, like the other pupils, he has learned to read and write Hebrew. David speaks English at home and he also knows some Arabic. In Israel the working week begins on Sunday and ends on Friday which is sometimes free, sometimes a half day. Saturday, called *Shabat*, is always a non-school, non-working day.

School begins at eight o'clock in the morning. David's lessons include math, history, geography, science, and Bible study. At one o'clock, David and the other pupils help to prepare lunch which they eat in the school dining room. He spends the afternoon with art lessons and private study until school finishes at three o'clock.

After school he enjoys playing soccer and volleyball with his friends. He is very interested in science and hopes to go to a technical high school where he can learn more about electronics.

New skills
Israel puts great stress on technological studies in schools so that the country can keep up with today's electronic world. All school children are encouraged to use computers and over half of them now choose to go to technical high schools.

Play and learn
Israel has the highest preschool attendance in the world. 97 percent of four-year-olds go to a playgroup or a nursery school. This is partly because many mothers go out to work and partly because the Israelis believe that children should begin to learn about life and mix with others from an early age.

The Jewish school system

Preschool
Playgroups

Primary schools
6–12

Junior schools
12–14

Technical schools 15–17	Agricultural schools 15–17	Secondary academic 15–17	Military schools 15–17	Religious schools 15–17

Army Service
Boys 18–21   Girls 18–20

College, Teacher training, Religious college, Art school

Arab schools

The Arabs have a separate school system in which pupils can study their own culture and religion. At one time only a small number of Arab girls were sent to school, but now they are nearly all in full-time education. The traveling Bedouin families are more difficult to teach since many of them move from place to place. Today, education for the Bedouin is available through a network of schools in their areas. Here is an Arab girls school in Jerusalem.

JERUSALEM – BEAUTY AND SORROW

Jerusalem is a beautiful city with a long and varied history. It is sacred to three of the world's great religions – Judaism, Christianity, and Islam. Within its massive walls there is a jumble of ancient buildings, religious sites, noisy alleyways, and bazaars (markets). It is a center of pilgrimage for people of many religions and it attracts tourists from all over the world. Jerusalem is also a thriving capital, seat of government, and center of the civil service and the law.

For centuries the old part of the city has been divided into different quarters: Arab, Jewish, Christian, and Armenian. At the cease-fire of 1949 the Old City was controlled by Israel's Arab neighbor, Jordan, and the Jews were not allowed entry. However, after the war of 1967 when Israel occupied the whole area, the sacred sites were once again opened to everyone.

Alongside historic Jerusalem is the New City, or West Jerusalem. This area grew up in the 20th century and contains all the features of a busy modern capital including the railroad station, the shopping center, and Israel's parliament, the Knesset.

The Via Dolorosa
"The Way of Sorrow" or Via Dolorosa marks the route that Jesus took from the place of his trial to Calvary, the place of his crucifixion. Each Friday, a procession retraces his steps to Calvary, where the Church of the Holy Sepulchre now stands. It is a place of pilgrimage for the world's Christians.

The Western Wall
The Western Wall (left) is all that remains of the Second Temple of Judaism which was destroyed by the Romans 2,000 years ago. It is the most sacred Jewish site in the world. Every day Jews gather here to pray, many of them dressed in the traditional clothing of Eastern European Jews – long black coats and broad-brimmed hats.

The Dome of the Rock

Jerusalem's skyline is dominated by the golden dome of the Mosque of Omar, sacred to Muslims. Inside it is a rock with a horse's hoofprint embedded in it. Muslims believe that it was from here that the Prophet Mohammed ascended to heaven in a mysterious night journey.

Tel Aviv

Tel Aviv (left) was Israel's first new town. It was begun in 1909 next to the ancient port of Yafo. Today it is a bustling modern city and the industrial and commercial center of the country. It is also a center for entertainment and the arts. Although Jerusalem was proclaimed Israel's capital in 1950, many governments still regard Tel Aviv as the capital.

EATING THE ISRAELI WAY

Food plays an important part in Jewish life. There are laws dating from ancient times which govern what may be eaten. Nowadays, not all Jews follow them but strong believers usually do. The laws state that only the meat from animals with cloven (divided) hooves that chew the cud may be eaten, so a Jew may not eat pork. Only fish with fins and scales are allowed so shellfish is forbidden. There is also a rule against the mixing of milk and meat and many households have separate utensils for these foods. Muslims also have special rules about their diet, but they are not the same as those of the Jews.

People from all over the world have settled in Israel, so Israeli cooking shows great variety. Some of the most popular dishes such as blintzes (stuffed pancakes) and gefilte fish (boiled fish balls) come from the traditional Jewish cooking of Eastern Europe. Nowadays, restaurants and hotels serve a wide range of Western as well as Jewish foods. Picnics, barbecues, and eating in sidewalk cafés are popular with Israelis everywhere.

Israeli fast food
Many foods associated with Israel are Arabic rather than Jewish. Felafel is one of these and is a great favorite. It consists of fried chick-pea balls with pickles and salad served in flat pita bread. It is usually sold and eaten on the street.

Jewish bread
At the beginning of the Sabbath on Friday evening, many Jewish families share a traditional meal. Plaited bread called *challah* is served. At the festival of Passover Jews do not eat anything with leaven (yeast) in it. Instead they eat a special unleavened bread called *matza*.

Old style

Fruit and vegetables are plentiful and cheap. They are produced in exotic variety. Colorful street markets like this can be found in every town. Goods can be sampled and prices compared.

Modern style

Supermarkets are a common sight today in Israel's towns. Imported American and European goods sit side by side with locally produced food on the shelves.

SPORTS AND PASTIMES

Sports of all kinds are growing in popularity with the Israelis. Physical education has become part of the school program and there are many sports clubs for teenagers.

Water sports are very popular. Swimming, snorkeling, windsurfing, and sailing are favorite pastimes with many. For such a warm country, skiing is also surprisingly popular. When the Golan Heights in the north came under Israeli control in 1967, the snowy slopes there became the home of the Israel Ski Club. Pony trekking and hang gliding are other examples of new sports to attract enthusiasts.

Israel belongs to the Asian Games Federation and also sends teams of athletes to the Olympic Games. Political problems are never far away and tragedy struck Israeli athletes at the 1972 Olympic Games in Munich, when the PLO killed 11 members of the Israeli team at the Games.

For many Israelis, archaeology is a consuming passion. With so many ancient sites to explore, many young people spend their summer vacations excavating the country's biblical past.

Swimming the lake

The warm climate of Israel encourages everyone to go swimming. One of the most popular events of the year is a 3 mile swim across Lake Kinneret (the Sea of Galilee). Each year thousands of dedicated swimmers, Israelis, and tourists alike, enjoy this test of stamina and skill.

Ballgames

Soccer, basketball, and volleyball are becoming increasingly popular in Israel. League games are supported by thousands of loyal fans. The Maccabi basketball team from Tel Aviv has won the European Cup Championships twice, in 1977 and 1981.

Tourism

More than a million tourists visit Israel each year. Half of them come from Europe and a third from North America. They are attracted by the warm climate, the varied scenery, and the wealth of historic sites. Approximately 100,000 people come as pilgrims to the holy places. Many young people visit Israel for the experience of living communally on a kibbutz. Here a group of tourists visit an ancient site.

Café society

All Israelis enjoy sitting and socializing in a café. Arab men have a long tradition of gathering in a coffee shop to exchange news over a cup of coffee, served in the Turkish manner, black and strong in small cups. Many of them enjoy smoking a waterpipe or playing the old game of backgammon.

HOUSES AND HOMES

The majority of Israelis are city dwellers. Housing has always been a problem for the rapidly-growing population and most people live in multi-story apartment complexes. There is, however, a wide variety of other kinds of houses from traditional Arab dwellings to modern architect-designed homes. Most apartments are compact, with a single living/dining room, a kitchen, bathroom, and two bedrooms. Solar heating is widely used.

The day starts early and most Israelis are at work or school by eight o'clock. The working day ends at three or four o'clock and there is a period of rest before the family gathers for the evening meal. Stores close during the hottest part of the day and re-open from four to seven. Some people like to shop in the late afternoon. After dinner, the evening may be spent watching television, doing homework, or enjoying hobbies. Most Jews, even those who are not religious, set aside Saturday (the Sabbath) as a family day.

Family life is important to both Jews and Arabs. Divorce rates are low (very low among Arabs) and while many Israeli women go out to work, many of them like to fill the traditional woman's role in the family.

Sun houses
These houses have a hot water supply heated by the sun's energy. The sun's warmth is trapped in special panels on the roof and heats water in tanks inside the house.

Faithful followers
The Jewish faith calls for its followers to organize their lives in a certain way. Not all Jews are religious, and some are more religious than others. Those who strictly observe the rules of the Jewish religion laid down in the Bible are called Orthodox Jews. They do their best to follow the laws of eating, praying, and studying. Orthodox families keep the Sabbath as a day of prayer and rest and celebrate all the religious festivals of the Jewish Year. Here a family follows the religious rules for eating together.

Bedouin tradition

Tent dwellers like these Bedouin can still be found in the south. The children may go to school and the family may use modern conveniences such as trucks and tractors but the Bedouin still live by old and proud traditions of behavior.

Children are expected to help with the work and to look after their younger brothers and sisters. Possessions are few and women still do most of the domestic chores.

KEY FACTS

▶ Most of Israel's population lives in the cities and towns.

▶ There are many new development towns being built in the less populated areas.

▶ The government gives financial help to people buying a house for the first time.

▶ Taxes in Israel are high. A large proportion of tax is spent on defense.

▶ The Histadrut is Israel's main trade union. It negotiates wage agreements and supplies a number of social services.

Close-knit families

Arab families tend to be close, with several generations often living under the same roof.

ARTISTS AND CRAFTSPEOPLE

Jews arriving in Israel from many parts of the world have brought with them their own kinds of music and dance. Israeli folk dances and songs have come mainly from Eastern Europe, while painting and sculpture have been influenced by the West. The Arab population also has its ancient traditions of arts and crafts. Local styles of craftwork in textiles, wood, and clay add to the rich mixture of artistic life to be found in Israel today.

A number of museums have been built since 1948. The Israel Museum in Jerusalem opened in 1965 and contains major collections of Jewish art, national archaeological treasures, and a modern sculpture garden. The Institute for Islamic Art is devoted to the art treasures of the Muslim world.

There are several theater groups who perform in Hebrew and other languages.

Musical excellence
During the 1930s, hundreds of Jewish musicians, composers, and singers were driven out of Europe by the threat of Nazism. Many came to Israel and as a result, new music schools were started and orchestras founded. The Israel Philharmonic Orchestra, which was formed in 1936, is now regarded as one of the finest in the world.

Sound and silence

Israel has a dance company which is unique in the world. It is made up of a mixture of deaf and hearing dancers. The hearing dancers give signs to their deaf partners through gesture and movement to indicate the rhythm and pace. Vibrations transmitted through the floor also act as signals to the deaf performers.

Age-old skills

The Arabs are well known for their intricate craftwork in many different materials. They excel in the making of textiles, carpets, jewelry, and pottery. These skills are kept alive in Israel today. Carved olive wood souvenirs such as the one above are one of their major sources of income. The carvings are popular with tourists, especially those visiting the religious sites at Nazareth and Bethlehem in the West Bank.

People of the book

The Israelis are great readers. Libraries and bookstores can be found in every city and town. Much modern literature and poetry is published in Hebrew. Every year there is a Hebrew book week which turns city squares and parks into crowded book markets. One of Israel's most distinguished writers is Shmuel Yosef Agnon who won the Nobel prize for literature in 1966.

CUSTOMS AND CELEBRATIONS

Not all citizens of Israel, whether Jewish, Muslim, or Christian, are religious, but most public holidays are based on religious festivals. Each group has its own holy day each week. For Muslims it is Friday, for Jews Saturday, and for Christians Sunday. Altogether there are about 40 public holidays a year, although they are not celebrated by everyone. Some of them, such as Independence Day, are not religious at all.

For Jews the year begins around September with Rosh Hashanah, the solemn New Year festival. After ten days comes Yom Kippur, the Day of Atonement, which is often spent in prayer asking God's forgiveness for sins. Pesach (Passover) is a spring festival when Jews celebrate the freeing of the Israelites from slavery in Egypt. Other celebrations include Chanukkah, (the Festival of Lights), which comes in winter and Sukkot, the Harvest Festival.

Weddings

Jewish weddings take place under a canopy called a *chuppah*. A rabbi (religious leader) conducts the ceremony. The bride and groom share a glass of wine during the service and the groom usually breaks the glass as a reminder of suffering in times of joy. Weddings are very festive occasions and are celebrated with food and drink, singing and dancing.

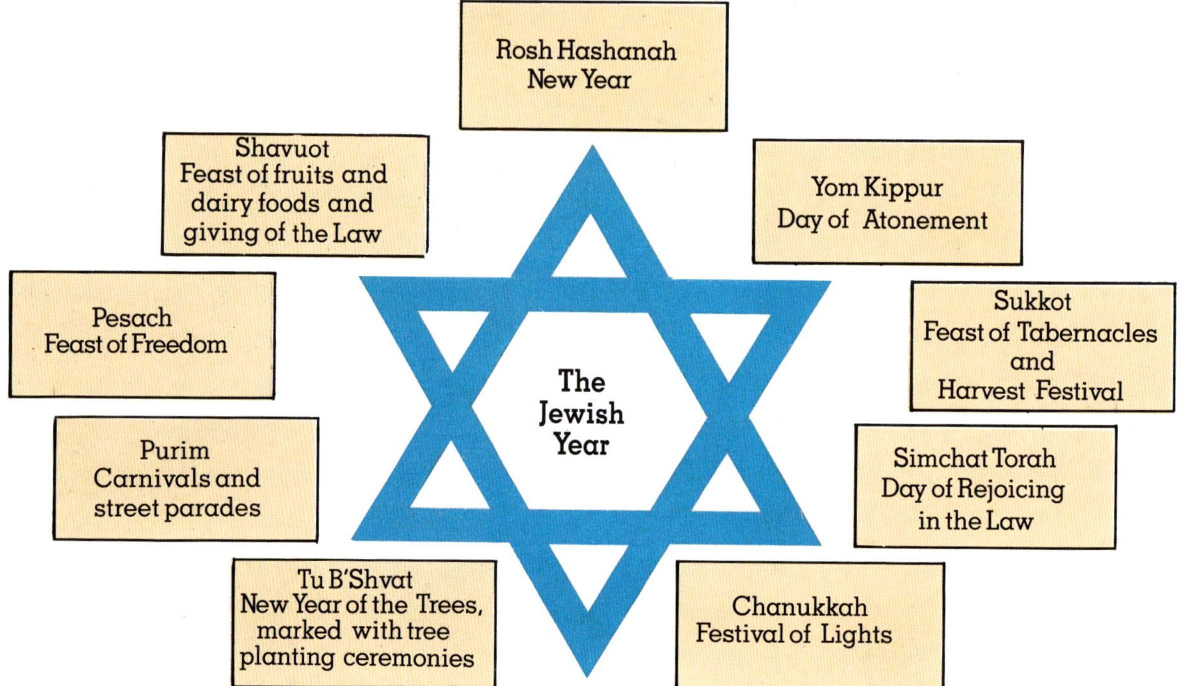

Carnival

In early spring, Jews celebrate
the festival of Purim. It is based
on a Bible story which tells
how a wicked courtier, Haman,
tried to destroy the Jews but
was killed himself. Today it is
celebrated with a carnival.
Special cakes called
Hamantaschen (Haman's ears)
are made, children dress up in
fancy dress and parade
through the street (above).

Fast and feast

Ramadan is the ninth month of
the Muslim year. During this
month, faithful Muslims (right)
devote themselves to fasting
and prayer. Nothing is eaten
between sunrise and sunset
during Ramadan. After dark,
families gather for the one
meal of the day. At the end of
the month, a celebration feast
is held as a thanksgiving.

A PEACEFUL FUTURE?

I srael is likely to face great challenges in the 1990s. Many long-standing problems have not been resolved and tension is mounting between the Palestinian Arabs and the Jews.

Although the Israelis work hard to make their country successful, much of their money is spent on defense. This causes financial difficulties and the people have to pay high taxes which will continue until peace is reached.

Many moderate Arabs and Jews want peace but cannot agree on a power-sharing system. The Palestinians want their own separate state in the occupied territories of the West Bank and Gaza. Most Israelis are not willing to trust them and will not agree to handing back the occupied areas. A solution to the problem is vital if more bloodshed is to be avoided. An international peace conference may be the only hope.

West Bank settlements
Some of the West Bank area is being developed with Israeli agricultural settlements. The Jewish settlers receive financial help from the government. The Arabs of the West Bank are resentful about the Israeli settlements because they believe that the settlements show that Israel intends to take over the West Bank forever. This would mean an end to Arab hopes of their own state in the West Bank. Tension in the area is mounting and causing international concern.

Here to stay

New apartments rise on the edge of old Jerusalem (left). They are built on land once controlled by Jordan. The flats show that Israel is determined to exist, in spite of the hostility of its Arab neighbors. New towns are a priority of the government and several are planned for the future.

Give peace a chance

Many individual Arabs and Jews would like to cooperate and live together peacefully, which is a hopeful sign for the future. Perhaps the children of this family at work in the cotton fields near Gaza will see peace in their lifetime.

Index

Acknowledgments

Map illustration by Ann Savage. All other illustrations by Linden Hamilton. Photographic credits (a = above, b = below, m = middle, l = left, r = right): Cover al Robert Harding Picture Library, bl Klaus Otto Hundt/BIPAC, ar Simon McBride/Hutchison Library, br Robert Harding Picture Library; page 7 Zefa; page 8 Simon McBride/Hutchison Library; page 9 a Robert Harding Picture Library; b Simon Lewis/BIPAC; page 11 Klaus Otto Hundt/BIPAC; page 12 Hutchison Library; page 13 a Hutchison Library, b Simon Lewis/BIPAC; page 14 BIPAC; page 15 Zefa; page 16 BIPAC; page 17 Klaus Otto Hundt/BIPAC; page 19 Robert Harding Picture Library; page 21 Hutchison Library; page 23 a BIPAC, b BIPAC; page 24 Robert Aberman/ Hutchison Library; page 25 Hutchison Library; page 26 Hutchison Library; page 27 a Frank D. Smith/BIPAC, b Hutchison Library; page 28 Hutchison Library; page 29 Havlicek/Zefa; page 31 Nancy Durrell McKenna/ Hutchison Library; page 32 Robert Harding Picture Library; page 33 a Robert Harding Picture Library, b Bernard Régent/Hutchison Library; page 35 a Robert Harding Picture Library, b Sipa-Press/Rex Features; page 37 Nancy Durrell McKenna/Hutchison Library; page 38 a Zefa, b W Braun/Zefa; page 39 Hutchison Library; page 40 BIPAC; page 43 Mark Halpern/BIPAC; page 44 Melani Friend/Hutchison Library; page 45 a Zefa, b Nancy Durrell McKenna/ Hutchison Library.